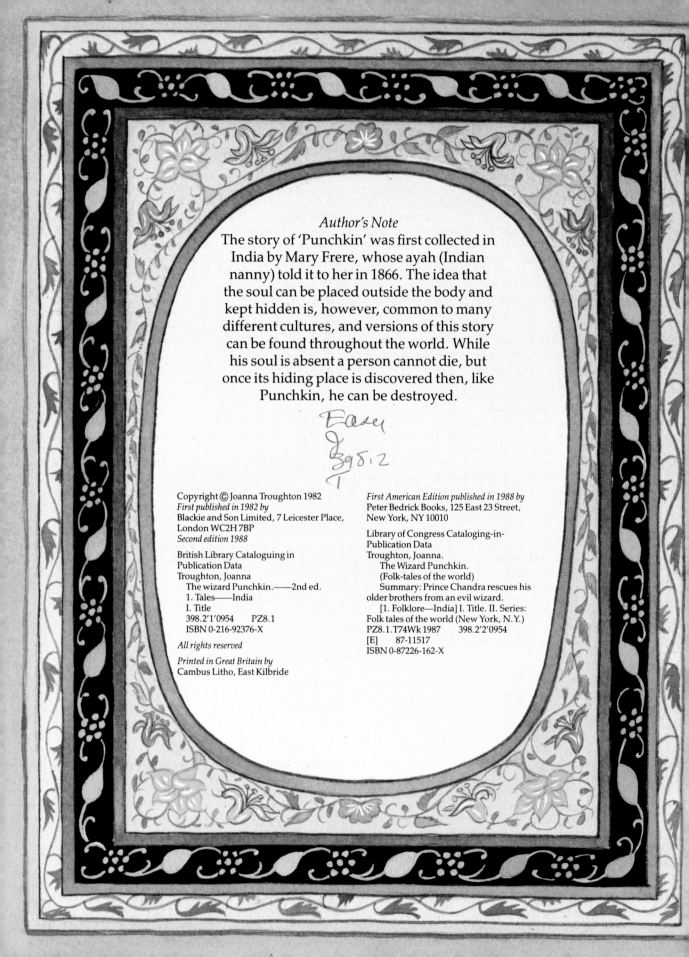

Author's Note

The story of 'Punchkin' was first collected in India by Mary Frere, whose ayah (Indian nanny) told it to her in 1866. The idea that the soul can be placed outside the body and kept hidden is, however, common to many different cultures, and versions of this story can be found throughout the world. While his soul is absent a person cannot die, but once its hiding place is discovered then, like Punchkin, he can be destroyed.

Easy
398.2
T

Copyright © Joanna Troughton 1982
First published in 1982 by
Blackie and Son Limited, 7 Leicester Place, London WC2H 7BP
Second edition 1988

British Library Cataloguing in Publication Data
Troughton, Joanna
  The wizard Punchkin.——2nd ed.
  1. Tales——India
  I. Title
  398.2'1'0954   PZ8.1
  ISBN 0-216-92376-X

Printed in Great Britain by
Cambus Litho, East Kilbride

First American Edition published in 1988 by
Peter Bedrick Books, 125 East 23 Street, New York, NY 10010

Library of Congress Cataloging-in-Publication Data
Troughton, Joanna.
  The Wizard Punchkin.
  (Folk-tales of the world)
  Summary: Prince Chandra rescues his older brothers from an evil wizard.
  [1. Folklore—India] I. Title. II. Series: Folk tales of the world (New York, N.Y.)
PZ8.1.T74Wk 1987   398.2'2'0954
[E]   87-11517
ISBN 0-87226-162-X

Folk Tales of the World

The Wizard
Punchkin

A Folk Tale from India

Retold and illustrated by

Joanna Troughton

BLACKIE
London

BEDRICK/BLACKIE
New York

There once lived in India a Rajah and Ranee, who had seven sons. One day the princes made ready to go hunting, but Chandra, the youngest, was forbidden to ride with his brothers.

"You are only a child," the Ranee said, "and the land is full of dangers."

"Hunt to the East, to the West and to the South," the Rajah advised his sons. "But do not hunt to the North, for there dwells the wicked wizard Punchkin."

But the six brothers paid little attention to their father's words as they rode away. Days passed; weeks passed, and finally years. The princes never returned.

Once Chandra was grown he had but one wish – to journey to the North, where the wizard Punchkin dwelt, for there he believed he would find his lost brothers. The Rajah and Ranee sadly agreed to let him go. And so, bidding his parents farewell, the young Prince set out on his search.

He had travelled for many days when he came upon a
serpent attacking a nest of young eagles. Quickly he
drew his bow, and with an arrow shot the serpent dead.
The parent eagles were so grateful that they gave
Chandra a magic feather which would summon them if
he should ever need their help.

Soon Chandra came to a stony wasteland, in the middle of which stood a palace with a tall tower. Among the rocks were statues – princes and noblemen, servants and hunting dogs. When Chandra looked closer, he saw the figures of his lost brothers!

"This must be an enchantment," he thought. "My brothers have been turned to stone and the same fate awaits me if I set foot upon this land. I must reach the palace and try to break this spell."

So Chandra wished upon his magic feather, and the father eagle came and carried the Prince safely over the wasteland. At a window in the tall tower was the most beautiful princess that Chandra had ever seen.
"Help me!" she cried. "My name is Laili. This palace belongs to the wizard Punchkin. He keeps me prisoner here until I promise to marry him."

Chandra asked the eagle to set him down near the tower, for he had fallen in love with Laili, and vowed to save her from the evil wizard.

"But Punchkin can never be killed," the Princess said. "Neither fire nor water nor steel can harm him, for he keeps his soul outside his body and has hidden it in a safe place."

"Then if we can find out where Punchkin's soul is hidden we shall have him in our power," Chandra replied. Suddenly there were footsteps on the stairs. "Quickly, hide!" said Laili.

It was the wicked wizard Punchkin!

"Are you willing to marry me yet, Princess?" asked Punchkin.

Laili sighed. "I can never be your wife while you keep secrets from me," she said. "I know that you hide your soul where no one can find it, but you have never told me where."

The wizard chuckled. "As you can never leave this palace my secret will be safe with you," he said. "So I will tell you, and then we shall be married."

And Punchkin told Laili where his soul was hidden. Chandra in his hiding place heard all the wizard's words. He sprang onto the eagle's back and away they flew.

Not far from the palace there was an ocean. In that ocean there was an island. On that island grew a jungle.

In that jungle stood a tree guarded by tigers. Hanging from that tree there was a cage. In that cage sat a parrot on a single egg. And in that egg was Punchkin's soul.

Down swooped the eagle, and Chandra seized the cage. Then back they flew to the wizard's palace.

When Punchkin saw the egg in Chandra's hand he was filled with terror.
"Give me back my soul!" he screamed. But Chandra squeezed the egg until it cracked.

And Punchkin died.

In the wasteland the spell was broken. Princes and noblemen, servants and hunting dogs came back to life.

Chandra was glad to see his lost brothers again. They all returned home.
"Punchkin is dead!" they told the Rajah and Ranee. And Chandra and Laili were married, and lived in great happiness.